CATWINGS
RETURN

Ursula K. Le Guin

CATWINGS RETURN

Illustrations by
S. D. SCHINDLER

A
LITTLE APPLE
PAPERBACK

SCHOLASTIC INC.
New York   Toronto   London   Auckland   Sydney

ISBN 0-590-42832-2

Text copyright © 1989 by Ursula K. Le Guin. Illustrations copyright © 1989 by S.D. Schindler. All rights reserved. Published by Scholastic Inc., 730 Broadway, New York, NY 10003, by arrangement with Orchard Books, a division of Franklin Watts, Inc. APPLE PAPERBACKS is a registered trademark of Scholastic Inc.

31 30 29 28 27 26 25 24 23 22 21   0 1/0

Printed in the U.S.A.   08

First Scholastic printing, March 1991

Also by

Ursula K. Le Guin

and S. D. Schindler

CATWINGS

CATWINGS
RETURN

Early on a rainy morning, Hank and Susan came over the hill at Overhill Farm to the old hay barn. High up in the wall of the barnloft were holes where pigeons used to fly in and out. Susan was looking up at those pigeonholes as she called, "Kit-kit-kit-kit-kittywings! Catwings! Breakfast!"

Out of a pigeonhole peeped — not a beak — but a cinnamon nose —

two round yellow eyes —

two white front paws —

and then, whooosh! out flew a cat. A cat with wings. A tabby cat with tabby wings.

The first one out was Thelma, always an early riser. Then came Roger, then (from a different pigeonhole) little Harriet, and finally James. He flew slower than the others, because

his left wing had been hurt once by an angry owl, but he joined them in their flying games, tumbling in the air all round the barn and driving the woodpeckers in the oak trees crazy. Then all at once all four cats came plummeting and loop-the-looping down with hungry mews and happy meows to breakfast.

Hank liked to toss kibbles in the air and watch Roger catch them, and Roger liked to catch them. Susan liked to hold kibbles in her hand while James ate them, tickling her fingers with his whiskers and purring loudly. Thelma and Harriet took their breakfast seriously, preferring not to play games with it.

So the children and the cats were all there that rainy morning in the old barn, when Hank said to his sister, "You know, I think Mother saw Roger yesterday. He was above the hill, in sight of the house."

"I think she saw them ages ago. *She* won't tell anybody!" Susan said, scratching Thelma's chin.

From the moment they discovered the flying tabbies, the children had known that they must keep them a secret. They feared people would want to put them in cages, in circuses or pet shows or laboratories, to make money by owning them or selling them.

"Of course Mother wouldn't tell!" Hank said. "But I'm glad nobody ever comes around this old barn."

"I think they understand about staying hidden," Susan said, tickling Harriet's fat little stomach. "After all, they were hiding in the woods when we found them. They were wild."

What Susan and her brother did not know was that the winged cats had not been born in the woods near Overhill Farm. They had come there from a long way off. They had been born in the city, under a dumpster in an alley, a wilder place than any woods.

After the children had left to catch the school bus, Thelma said, "I wonder how our mother is! I think about her every day."

"I still miss her," Roger said.

"I do too," said James.

"Let's go back and see her!" said Harriet.

"Oh, no," Roger said seriously. "Too many people in the city—it's dangerous. Mother told us to use our wings to escape, and we did. We should stay where we're safe."

"Mother would be so pleased," Harriet

argued, and James said, "We could just make a flying visit!"

Thelma shook her head. She agreed with Roger. When the other two went on talking about it, she said, "It might be a hard flight for you, James."

"But I'm hardly lame at all now," James replied, waving both his wings gracefully in proof. "And we weren't much more than kittens when we flew all that way before. I'd like to see the old alley just one more time!"

"Remember the lovely smelly sardine cans in the garbage?" Harriet said.

"Remember how you flew up and scared that huge dog?" James said.

So James and Harriet made up their minds to go visit their mother, Mrs. Jane Tabby, in the city. Thelma and Roger chose to stay home with their friends Susan and Hank. "Think how sad the children would be," said Roger, "if they came tomorrow and we were all gone!"

And indeed the children were worried when they came to the old barn next morning and found two of the flying tabbies missing. They called and called for them. Roger and Thelma purred twice as much as usual, but could not explain where their brother and sister had gone. So all of them there in the old barn were anxious, thinking about Harriet and James, and wondering, "Where are they now? Will they come back safe?"

2

HARRIET and James were flying along through a fine, soft rain. When daylight came, they were glad of the rain and clouds that hid them from sight as they flew. As James said, "Nobody looks up when it's raining!"

Looking down, Harriet saw hills and fields and roads below them, but she did not see the city.

"I think we should be going more to the left, James," she called through the raindrops.

"Why?" James asked, flying closer.

"My Instinct tells me so," said Harriet. "We have to trust our Homing Instinct. It will take us straight back to the place where we were born!"

James was impressed. He followed his sister. But at last, when they were resting on a branch of a big tree, he said, "Harriet, we've been flying for hours. Shouldn't we at least have *seen* the city by now?"

"Maybe it moved," Harriet said.

"Of course I'm a slow flyer," James said gloomily.

"You're just as fast as I am," his sister said, also gloomily. "Maybe my Instinct is out of practice. What does your Instinct tell you?"

"It doesn't say anything," James replied. "But my *nose* — my nose says something *stinks* — in *that* direction!"

Harriet lifted her cinnamon nose and sniffed. She half opened her mouth, to smell the smells only cats can smell. A puff of wind blew by. "Aha!" she said. "Garbage! That's it!"

So they flew on, resting on a treetop or a roof when they were tired, waking in the depths of the night and flying on again. They could see well enough, for the lights of the great city ahead of them made all the cloudy sky glow with a dull yellowish light. When morning came again, there was nothing beneath them but rain-wet roofs and deep streets crowded

with shiny car-tops and umbrellas, mile after mile after mile.

James said nothing, but his left wing ached, and he wished they had not come.

Harriet said nothing, but both her wings ached, and she wished they had not come.

They sniffed the wind, and whether it was their Homing Instinct that guided them, or their noses that recognized the familiar smells, they flew slowly past all the high office buildings and apartment houses to the narrowest, dirtiest alley in the oldest, poorest part of the city. There they alighted on the corner of a roof, folded their wings, and looked down.

"This can't be our alley, James," Harriet whispered. "Where's the dumpster?"

They both thought of that dumpster, which they had been born under and played in as kittens, as their home. And it was gone.

"I don't know. Everything looks strange,"

James whispered back. "But I'm sure this is the place. Aren't you?"

Harriet nodded. "But if the dumpster's gone," she said in a very small voice, "where's Mother?"

After a long silence, James said only, "We'd better find something to eat, so that we can think clearly."

The windows of the old apartment house they sat on were all broken, and the empty rooms inside were a-scurry with mice. Breakfast was no problem.

After breakfast, sitting up on the roof again in the thin, weak sunshine that had followed the rain, the tabbies washed their faces, as their mother had taught them. They had a short nap, curled up close together.

Strange noises woke them — roaring, grinding, crashing, hammering, men shouting, metal screaming against stone. They peered over the edge of the roof and saw a fearful sight. An old building at the far end of the alley was being bashed and battered by a huge metal ball swinging from a crane, till the walls opened and the floor collapsed and the whole house fell apart into fragments and dust.

James was so terrified that he held perfectly still, hiding his eyes with his paw. But Harriet's fear made her leap up into the air and fly back and forth across the alley, crying wildly, "Mother! Where are you? Mother, we're here! We're here! Where are you, Mother?"

3

Nobody heard Harriet's little voice. Nobody paid any attention. Terrified rats and mice and beetles scurried from the foundations of the destroyed building. A couple of city pigeons flew by to see what the cloud of dust was. "Knocking down another slum," one pigeon said, and the other said, "That's progress," and they flew on. The men and machines in the alley moved to the next building and began getting it ready to be destroyed. Nobody had seen Harriet flitting above the rooftops, and at last, weeping, she came back to James.

"Help me call to her, James!" she said.

They stood side by side at the edge of the roof, and both called as loudly as they could:

"*Mother!*"

Then they listened.

The machinery had stopped roaring. The deserted buildings were all silent. The men were sitting around on their machines and in the ruins, eating lunch from their lunchboxes. No cars came down the rubble-choked street. It was quite still there inside the endless roar of the city all around. And in that stillness, James and Harriet heard a tiny voice.

"Me!" it wailed. "Me! Meeeee!"

James's eyes grew round and bright.

Harriet's tail lashed.

Both of them looked across the alley at a dark dormer window in the roof of an old warehouse.

"That's not Mother's voice," Harriet whispered.

They stared. Something moved inside the dark window — something black.

"Probably a starling's nest," James said. "Starlings make queer noises. I'll go see." And he darted quick as a swallow across the air between the roofs.

Harriet saw him land on the top of the dormer and fold his wings. Then slowly, paw by paw, flowing along the way he did when he was hunting, he came around to the broken window and peered in.

In another moment he was back beside her. "It's a kitten!" he said. "A black kitten— all by itself. It saw me and hissed and hid."

"But its mother must be somewhere around!" said Harriet.

"I don't know. I couldn't see inside. But I didn't smell anybody else."

"How would a kitten get up there by itself?"

"Its mother must have carried it up the stairs."

"But those machines are knocking down all the houses!" Harriet cried. She did not understand, or care, that the machines only did what the men told them to do. "They'll knock down that house too! With the kitten in it! We have to *do* something, James!" And she opened out her striped wings.

"Don't let them see you," James said.

"I won't." And she flew across to the other roof as he had done, very straight and fast, so that anyone looking up would hardly have time to see her. She landed on the roof in front of the dormer and looked in. After a moment, James joined her.

The attic of the warehouse was deserted and almost bare. There were no floorboards, only beams with insulating paper between

19 :

them. A few old crates and cardboard cartons lay in the corners. It smelled of dust and very ancient rat-droppings — and a thin, milky, warm, little smell of kitten.

"Don't be afraid," Harriet called softly. "We've come to help you!"

Silence.

"Won't you come out?" James called.

Silence.

James and Harriet moved away from the broken window, around the corners of the dormer. One on each side of the dormer, like library lions, they lay down on their stomachs with their front paws folded under their chests. They half closed their eyes. And they waited. Cats are patient. Even when they are anxious and frightened, they will wait quietly, watching to see what happens.

For a long time, nothing happened. The men and machines down in the alley finished pushing dust and rubble around for the day.

The men went away. The machines sat waiting, more quietly even than the cats, but much more stupidly.

Just as the lights were coming on in the endless streets of the city, something moved at the dormer window. A small face peered out. The kitten came cautiously with a little jump over the broken glass in the window frame. It went straight to the puddle of rain water in the gutter at the edge of the roof. There it crouched and drank thirstily, lapping and lapping. It was very small, very thin, with ragged-looking fur, black from nose to tailtip, all black, even its small, dusty, folded wings.

Harriet and James watched it in perfect silence, one on each side of the dormer.

The kitten turned to slink back into the attic, its hiding place—and saw them.

It gave a jump of terror. Then its back arched—its short black tail puffed up—its little wings spread out and flapped—its yellow eyes glared like headlights—and showing its tiny white kitten-teeth, it shouted bravely at them: "HATE! HATE! HATE!"

Harriet and James sat quite still. James smiled. Harriet purred.

The kitten stared wildly from one to the other and then, with a flying leap, returned to its attic. They could hear it scramble across the beams to hide in one of the cartons.

Harriet moved down the roof, and so did James, till they met in front of the broken window. There they sat down. James washed Harriet's right ear, and Harriet leaned her head against his shoulder.

"Is your poor old wing sore, after all that flying?" she asked.

"Not very. I hope we can find Mother soon," said James. They both spoke loud enough that the kitten inside the attic could hear them.

"Mother must have found a new place to live, when they took away the dumpster."

"But she wouldn't go far away, I'm sure."

"Not if she had a kitten here!"

"Mother would never leave a kitten alone for one moment longer than she had to."

"She *always* came back to us, when we were little."

"Of course she did. And when I got lost, remember? — chasing a sparrow, before I could fly very well—she found me hiding in the back seat of an old wrecked car—"

"And she picked you up by the nape of the neck and brought you home! Yes, I remember! *What* a scolding! And then she washed you all over twice."

"And purred....Remember how Mother always purred us to sleep?"

"Yes. Like this." And Harriet began to sing a purring lullaby, and James joined her, loud and low, loud and low...until at the broken window a little, fierce, frightened, black face appeared, staring at them.

Harriet and James seemed not to notice. They began talking again.

"I'm sure Mother is all right, Harriet. She knows how to look after herself, living in this alley all her life."

"I know. And families do get separated in bad times. But they find each other again."

"But of course Mother can't fly. So it's easier for *us* to find *her*—because we have wings."

"Poor Mother!" Harriet said sorrowfully.

Behind her a tiny voice wailed — "Meeee!" The kitten was crying.

Harriet made the soft noise, "Prrrrt!" that her mother used to make when she came back to the dumpster. She got up, turned very quietly to the window, and began to wash the kitten's ears. The kitten held still, trembling.

"How about a little something to eat?" said James cheerfully, and flew off.

He was back in a few minutes with a catch

from the empty rooms of the warehouse. Harriet was going to eat just a bite or two, but she didn't get a chance. The starving kitten growled, pounced, and carried the dinner off into the attic, where it ate every bite.

Later, when the kitten was sound asleep in the big cardboard box, curled up against James's warm, furry side, Harriet went hunting for her own supper. But she brought nearly half of it back for the kitten's breakfast.

All that night and the next day and night they stayed with the kitten. They curled up with it in its carton, and talked, and purred, and washed, and slept. The kitten needed a great deal of washing. Harriet whispered to James, "The poor little thing has *fleas*, James!" (The fleas were not happy about all this washing. Several of them left to seek a more restful residence.) After some good meals and a lot of washing and purring, the kitten did not look so scrawny and ragged. But still it cowered and hissed whenever a board creaked, and still it would not talk. It could not tell James and Harriet how it had gotten lost, or where its mother might be. All it could say was its sad little cry of "Me!" and its defiant hiss of "HATE!"

In the evening and early morning James and Harriet took turns flying out to scout the neighborhood for sight or word of Mrs. Jane Tabby. But there wasn't a cat left anywhere near the alley. Nor a dog. Nor a human being, except for the workmen in the daytime. Only the mice and rats and beetles and fleas, who didn't know where else to go, and the machines. In the daytime, the crane with its wrecking-ball moved closer and closer to the warehouse.

Concerned with the kitten and worried about finding their mother, James and Harriet forgot to pay attention to the crane. They did not keep watch on it. They were all dozing

together in the carton when the crane moved to
stand in front of the very building they were in,
and the huge metal ball swung out and bashed
a gaping hole in the front wall. Then, in a
panic, James rushed to the dormer window,
crying, "Fly, Harriet! Fly!"

The kitten cowered hissing and spitting
with terror in the corner of the carton. Harriet

wasted no time arguing with it. She closed her accurate, gentle jaws right on the nape of the kitten's neck, picked it up, and ran across the beams to the window. She flew out, the kitten dangling between her paws, just as the destroyer struck again. The whole building shook and tottered, and the floors fell.

Above her James circled, calling, "This way, Harriet!"

She followed him blindly through the dust-cloud.

Down in the alley, the crane operator looked up into the dust and blinked several times. "Birds," he said. "They *had* to be birds."

Later on, eating a ham sandwich out of his tin lunchbox, he asked his friend who was sitting on the same heap of bricks, "Did you ever see a bird that had whiskers? And front feet?"

"Nope," said the other man. "Can't say I ever did. Want a dill pickle?"

4

AT FIRST the kitten hung perfectly still and obedient, letting Harriet hold it. But it was not a baby, and before long it began to struggle and twist, trying to get free. Harriet was a small cat, not used to carrying a half-grown kitten while she flew. As the kitten struggled, her flight wobbled, and she beat her wings hard trying to keep on course. Then the kitten twisted right round and broke free—above a street crowded with whizzing cars! Down it dropped—Harriet frantically trying to pursue it—James desperately trying to fly under it to break its fall—down—down—until all at once the little black wings spread out wide and began to beat the air, and the kitten soared up, up, over the cars, past the telephone wires, above the roofs, and flew.

Thankful but furious, James and Harriet flew after it. "Wait!" they shouted. "Kitten! Wait!"

Quite soon, out of breath and strength, the kitten began to falter and fly lower. James did fly under it then, and let it alight on his back, between his wings. Then he glided straight for the nearest flat roof. And there the three of them crouched, panting and exhausted.

A starling whose nest was up in the chimney top looked down at them. "Hey!" she said indignantly. "Clear out! We don't need any more of you crazy cats on roofs!"

"Cats?" said James. "Tell us where the other cats are, and we'll go!"

"Next street over," said the starling, cocking her head. "With the flowerpots." She made a rude noise.

"Thank you," said Harriet with dignity. "Kitten, come now. We shall look for Mother."

The street the starling had indicated was a quiet one, though not deserted like the old alley. One small poodle yipped sadly behind a closed window as the cats flew past. No people walked on the sidewalks.

"Mother!" James called.

"Mother!" Harriet called.

And the kitten, flying bravely between them, squeaked, "Meeee!"

Then a voice replied from above them, a soft, clear, well-remembered voice.

"Children?"

They looked up, and flew to her.

On the flat roof of the tallest apartment house in the street stood a little penthouse, like a cottage, with a garden on the roof all around it — growing in pots and tubs, but a garden all the same. And there, among the pots and tubs and watering cans and wash-lines, was their mother, Mrs. Jane Tabby, purring with joy.

"My dear Harriet! My dear James! And my poor, little, lost kitten!" Mrs. Jane never cried, but her purr was rather shaky as she kissed them all. She began at once to wash the kitten's neck and ears, but as she did so she said, "Are you all right, my dears? You look very well; you have grown up very handsome. And Thelma? And Roger?"

"We're all just fine, Mother —"

"We live in a barn loft in the country —"

"Nobody comes there, no human beings, I mean —"

"Except two very nice young ones, who feed us and pet us —"

"But, Mother, what about you? How did you leave the alley?"

"How did the kitten get lost?"

Harriet and James could not ask questions fast enough, until their mother began to speak. As she spoke, she curled round the black kitten, who, worn out, was already falling asleep.

"Well, my dears, that was the worst day of my life. And since that day until this moment, I
have been very sad, thinking my last little kitten

was lost! She was my only child, born not long before the street began to fall down. Her father was Mr. Tom Jones. You remember him, I'm sure."

Harriet and James nodded.

"She looks like him," their mother said with pride. "But he was called by business to another part of town. And before he returned, a dreadful thing happened. The dumpster, my lifelong home, was taken away. And while I was camping behind the trash cans, people saw the kitten — saw her trying out her wings, just as you children used to do — climbing to the top of the trash cans and flying back down. The human beings got excited, making terrible noises, shouting and yelling. They ran to catch her — I ran to defend her. We were separated! The poor baby, given strength by her terror, flew straight up and into a broken window high on a roof. I could not follow her. The people could not enter the building; it was locked.

They were angry, and in their anger they pursued me. I ran, in such terror that I lost my way."

"Oh, Mother!" Harriet whispered, and James trembled, listening.

"For hours I wandered, calling to my kitten. Dogs chased me. At last, when I was half dead with weariness, hands suddenly picked me up. I scarcely knew what was happening, as I was carried indoors and up many stairs, and set down at last, here. And here I have been ever since! I have a true friend in the kind old woman whose hands picked me up. She feeds and pets me, and her lap is most comfortable. I am too old to enjoy street life any more, and I would have been very happy here, but for the thought of my poor lost kitten. The door to the stairway is locked, and I could find no way down to look for her. But now you, my dear, dear children, have saved her and brought her back to me!"

The black kitten was fast asleep. Mrs. Jane led Harriet and James over to a large food dish well stocked with kibbles, and a bowl of clear water. When they had eaten and drunk, she spoke again.

"Do you think the kitten can fly well enough to go back to your country home with you?"

"I think so," said James, "if she'll ride on my back part of the time."

"And on my back too," said Harriet. "But we don't want to take her from you again, Mother—"

"Oh, my dears, she must go," said Mrs. Jane. "Now that I know she is alive and well, and is with those who will look after her, all I wish is that she be safe. And there is no place in this city for a winged cat to be safe. You know that, children."

Sadly, Harriet and James nodded.

: 40

"Take her with you, and I will be content,"

said Mrs. Jane. "I will lie in the sun in my
roof-garden and dream of her flying with you,
in freedom. And that will be my happiness."

Then for the last time they all curled up
together, the kitten and the young cats and the
mother, and purred each other to sleep with
the lullaby loud and low, loud and low.

5

THE FIRST night of the journey home was the hardest. The black kitten flew valiantly as far as she could, but her wings were short, and she had been weakened by her days without food in the warehouse attic. Soon she had to ride on James's back, and then on Harriet's. Then all of them, worn out, had to find a roof to rest on. Then they would fly on again, but before long they had to come down and rest again. And there seemed no end to the city, or to the night.

Deep in his heart, James was afraid they could not find the way back to Overhill Farm. Deep in her heart, Harriet was afraid of the same thing. Neither of them admitted it. They flew forward cheerfully, hoping that their Homing Instinct knew what it was doing.

"James!" Harriet called, pointing a paw downward. "Remember that roof?"

It was a church roof, and Harriet had sat on the top of the steeple when she was only a kitten herself, flying away from the city with her brothers and sister.

"Yes! I do! We *are* going the right direction!" James shouted. He was so excited

that he flew a circle around the church spire.

The black kitten was scared and dug her little needle-claws into his back to hold on. "It's all right, kitten!" James said. "Hang on now. We're going home!"

THELMA sat on the high ridgepole of the old barn at Overhill. It was after sunset. The western sky was gold above the hills. But Thelma looked eastward.

Roger sat on the highest branch of a great oak on the hill behind the barn. Anyone seeing him would have thought he was an owl, waiting motionless for the dark. He was looking eastward.

Up on the top of the hill, Hank and Susan sat side by side, saying nothing. They had been in the woods for an hour, calling Harriet and James.

All at once Thelma flew up from the barn roof and Roger from the oak, calling, "There they are! They're coming!"

And the tired, hungry travelers flew slowly
down out of the darkening sky, to be greeted
with great joy by their brother and sister. Hank
and Susan came running down the hill, calling,
"Harriet! James! Where *were* you? Oh, James!
Oh, Harriet!"

And then everybody was in the barnyard
looking at the little black kitten.

"Mother sent her to live with us," said
James, and Harriet said, "She is our little
sister!"

The kitten looked around at everyone.
When she looked at Hank and Susan, her
back began to arch and her black fur to stand

up, and she spread her beautiful little wings as
if to fly. Then she sat down and scratched one
ear. Then she fell over on her side and
wriggled, looking sideways at Susan. "Me?"
she said.

Everybody laughed.

"She needs milk!" Hank cried, and jumped
up, and was off like an arrow. When he came
back in five minutes with a jar of fresh milk,
the kitten was flying somersaults and chasing
moths all over the barnyard. Susan sat with
weary James and Harriet on her lap, telling

them what noble cats they were and how much everyone had missed them.

"Here, kitty-kitty-kittywings!" Hank called, pouring the jar lid full of creamy milk. "No, Roger, wait till the kitten's had some. What's its name, I wonder?"

"Me?" cried the kitten, diving straight at the milk.

"Mimi?" said Hank.

"I don't think so," Susan said, gazing at the kitten. "I think...I think her name might be Jane."

The kitten stopped lapping milk at once and looked up. "ME!" she said in a loud, happy voice. Then she began to lap again, spattering drops of milk all over her little black face.

"O.K.," Hank said, "I guess she's Jane!"

"Of course she is," said Thelma. "Drink your milk now, Jane, and then for a bath and

bed. It's been a long, long day for a kitten!"